Development: Kent Publishing Services, Inc.
Design and Production: Signature Design Group, Inc.
Illustrations: Jan Naimo Jones

SADDLEBACK PUBLISHING, INC.
Three Watson
Irvine, CA 92618-2767

Website: www.sdlback.com

ISBN 1-56254-784-4

Printed in the United States of America

1 2 3 4 5 6 08 07 06

Chapter 1

Clay was on his way to lunch. He thought about the next football game. It was on Friday night. Carter High would play Glen High.

Clay was the starting quarterback.

Clay saw Dan. Dan was at his locker.

Dan said, "Wait, Clay. I will walk to lunch with you."

Clay stopped walking. He waited for Dan.

Clay and Dan were good friends now. But they hadn't been good friends last year.

Dan put his books in his locker.

Then he came over to Clay. They walked down the hall.

Dan said, "I can hardly wait for Friday night to come."

Dan was on the football team too. He was a running back. He was also the back-up quarterback.

Dan had wanted the job as starting quarterback last year. But Clay had gotten it. Dan had helped him get it.

Clay was new to the school last year. And he didn't know all of the Carter High plays.

Coach Grant asked Dan to help Clay learn some of the plays. Dan didn't want to help Clay. But he did help Clay. Dan's help got Clay the job.

Dan said, "I hope we beat Glen High. But Glen High has a good team. And I am not sure we can beat them. What do you think?"

Clay said, "We can beat them. I feel good about this year. I think we will win all of our games. We will even win the Hillman game. It won't be easy. But I think we will be number one in the state this year."

Clay also thought he might make the All-State team.

Dan said, "I hope we will be number one. We haven't lost a game so far. But I am not sure we can beat Glen High and Hillman High."

"Don't worry, Dan. We will beat them," Clay said.

"I sure hope you are right," Dan said.

Clay saw Kim. She was walking down the hall.

Clay asked Kim for a date last year, but she wouldn't date him.

Kim smiled at Clay.

She said, "Hi, Clay."

"Hi," Clay said.

And he smiled back at Kim.

Was Kim just being friendly? Or did she want to date him now?

Clay wished he knew. He still wanted to date Kim.

Clay had seen Kim only a few times this year. But she had spoken to him each time. He was always on his way to class or to lunch. So he didn't have time to talk to her. Clay wished Kim had lunch when he did. Then he might be able to talk to her in the lunch line.

Clay could call her at home, but he wouldn't do that. Not after she turned him down for a date last year.

"Maybe Kim wants to date you," Dan said.

"Maybe," Clay said.

Clay could ask Kim for a date. And then he would know for sure. But he wouldn't ask her unless he thought she might say yes.

Clay asked, "Does Kim have a boyfriend?"

"I don't know. Why? Do you want to date her?" Dan asked.

"Maybe," Clay said.

"I will ask Eve. Maybe she will know. Eve will find out for you. She is on the volleyball team, and Kim is on the team too," Dan said.

Eve was Dan's girlfriend.

"Don't tell Eve I want to know," Clay said.

Dan laughed.

Then he said, "You know I have to tell her that, or she might think I want to date Kim. But I will tell her not to tell Kim that you want to know."

Dan was a good friend. Clay was glad he and Dan were friends now.

Chapter 2

It was Thursday. Clay, Kirk, and Dan were at football practice. Dan and Kirk had just walked out on the field.

Kirk was Dan's best friend. Kirk was on the tennis team. But Kirk also helped with the football team.

Dan ran over to Clay.

Dan said, "I asked Eve about Kim. She said Kim doesn't have a boyfriend now."

Clay was glad to hear that.

"Thanks for finding out for me," Clay said.

"Sure. See you later," Dan said.

Dan ran over to talk to Kirk. And Hank ran over to talk to Clay.

Hank was the number three quarterback. It was Hank's first year on the team. He hoped to be the starting quarterback next year. He told Clay that on the first day of practice.

Hank said, "I can hardly wait until tomorrow night. Glen High has a good team. I know it will be hard to beat them. And I am only the number three quarterback. But do you think Coach Grant will let me play?"

Clay knew Hank wanted him to say yes. But he wasn't going to lie to Hank. It wouldn't be fair to Hank.

Clay said, "He might let you play. But we will have to score a lot of points first."

"I sure hope we score a lot. And that isn't just because I want to play. I want to win too," Hank said.

Coach Grant blew his whistle.

Then Coach Grant said, "Get started on your exercises. We have a lot to do today."

The boys did their exercises. Then Clay, Dan, and Hank practiced passing for a little while.

Clay passed well. But he often passed well. Dan passed better than last year. But Hank didn't pass well.

Coach Grant blew his whistle again.

He said, "We will play a game first. Then we will talk about the Glen High team."

The boys started to play a game. Clay passed well. Dan ran well. The team quickly scored a touchdown.

"Good job, boys," Coach Grant said.

The team scored two more touchdowns. Then the coach took Clay

out. Dan was now the quarterback. Dan helped the team score two more touchdowns.

Then the coach let Hank play. But Hank didn't play well. And the team didn't score any more points.

Coach Grant said, "Time to stop. We need to talk about Glen High."

Coach Grant talked about the good runner on the Glen High team. Then he talked some more about the team.

Carter High had worked on some new plays. Coach Grant talked about the new plays too.

Then he said, "Get to bed early tonight. Get a lot of rest. I want you to be in good shape for the game. The Glen High team will be hard to beat. But you can beat them."

All of the boys cheered.

Then Coach Grant said, "Be ready to play on Friday night. I plan on us being number one in the state this year."

All of the boys cheered again. They all wanted to be number one too.

Chapter 3

It was Friday night. The game was about to start. The Carter High team was in the locker room.

Clay talked to Dan.

Clay said, "I am ready for the game to start. We can beat Glen High. I am sure of that."

"I hope you are right," Dan said.

Then Coach Grant talked to the team.

He said, "Keep your mind on the game. Don't forget what you did in practice. And play your best. This won't be an easy win. But we can win this game."

The team cheered.

Then Coach Grant said, "Now get out on the field. You need to do some warm-up exercises."

The team ran out of the locker room on to the field. They did some exercises.

The Glen High team ran out on the field too. They did some exercises.

Then both teams ran and practiced their passes and tackles.

Coach Grant blew his whistle. All of the Carter boys ran over to him.

Coach Grant said, "It is time for the game to start. So don't forget what I said. Play your best. It won't be easy, but we can win this game."

All of the Carter boys cheered.

The referee blew his whistle.

Then he said, "Captains, come over here."

Clay and Dan were the co-captains. They ran over to the referee. Two boys from Glen High ran over to him too.

The referee said, "I will toss a coin. Glen High can call the toss."

He tossed the coin. A Glen High boy called heads. But it was tails.

Then the referee looked at Clay and Dan.

He said, "Do you want to kick? Or do you want to receive?"

"Receive," Clay said.

Clay knew Coach Grant always liked to have the ball first.

The referee said, "Glen High will kick first. Carter High will receive."

Clay and Dan ran back over to the Carter High team.

Coach Grant said, "It is time to play, boys. Get out on the field. Show those Glen High boys how to play."

All of the Carter boys cheered again.

Then the starting team ran out on the field.

Clay said, "We can win this. So play your best."

Glen High kicked the ball. Dan got the ball on the ten-yard line. He ran it back to the twenty. Then a Glen High player tackled him.

Clay said, "Now let's get ahead and stay that way."

On the next play Clay threw a ten-yard pass. The team got a first down.

Clay passed some more. The team slowly moved down the field.

Carter High got to the two-yard line. Then Clay ran over for a touchdown.

The Carter team cheered loudly. The Carter fans cheered too.

Then Carter made the extra point.

Carter High 7, Glen High 0.

The Carter team ran off the field.

Coach Grant said, "Great job, boys. Keep playing well."

Clay scored one more touchdown. Then Dan scored a touchdown. Another Carter boy scored a touchdown too.

Dan also ran for a lot of yards.

But Glen High played well too.

The final score was Carter High 26, Glen High 19.

Chapter 4

It was Monday. Clay and Dan were in Mrs. Vance's English class.

It was almost time for class to start.

Dan sat next to Clay. He looked over at Clay.

He said, "You played a great game Friday night, Clay."

"Thanks. So did you," Clay said.

Dan said, "I didn't think we could do it. But you were right. It wasn't easy, but we beat Glen High. I think we will win this week too. But it should be an easy win."

"I think it will be too," Clay said.

The next game was with Walker High. It was a home game. The

Hillman game was the next week. And then the team had two away games.

The bell rang.

Mrs. Vance said, "Get out your homework. We need to go over it first."

Clay got his homework out. He thought he did well on it. But he wasn't sure he got it all right.

Mrs. Vance said, "The first person in row one will start. Then we will go down the row. And then on to the first person in the next row. Tell me what word you put in the sentence. Then read the sentence."

The class went over the homework. Clay got a B on it.

Then Mrs. Vance said, "I won't grade you today. But I will grade you tomorrow. Do the next page for homework. It is the same as your work today. So you should all make a good grade."

Clay had a lot to do after school. He had hoped they wouldn't have any homework.

Mrs. Vance said, "Now we need to talk about your paper."

"What paper?" Clay asked.

Mrs. Vance said, "You have to write a three-page paper. It should be about a person you admire. Go to the school media center and use one or two books to find out about the person. Your paper should be in your own words. Don't copy straight from the book."

Clay asked, "When do we have to turn the paper in?"

Clay had a lot to do. He hoped it wouldn't be soon.

"Friday," Mrs. Vance said.

"Friday? It is due that soon?" Clay asked.

Mrs. Vance said, "Yes. You are

seniors now. We have a lot to do this year."

Clay did have a lot of work to do.

The Walker High game was on Friday night. It should be an easy win. But Clay wanted to rest the night before the game. He wanted to go to bed early. But he might have to stay up late to finish his paper.

Clay decided he would get up early tomorrow morning. Then he could go to the media center before school started. He wouldn't have time to go after school.

Clay needed to start on his paper as soon as he could. That way he could finish it before Thursday.

Chapter 5

It was the next morning. Clay had just gotten to school. He was early. Classes wouldn't start for an hour.

Clay went to the media center. He saw Kim. She was looking at some books on a shelf. He wished he had time to talk to Kim. But he was there to work, not to talk.

Clay saw Dan.

Dan walked over to Clay. He had a book in his hand.

Clay said, "I can guess why you are here. You are working on the paper for Mrs. Vance."

Dan said, "Yeah. I knew I should do this now. I didn't want to wait until the last minute. I want to go to bed early on Thursday night. Then I won't be tired on Friday night. I want to be ready for the Walker High game."

"That is why I am here too," Clay said.

"I found a book. I had better get to work," Dan said.

Dan went to a table and sat down. Clay looked for what he needed.

Clay found a book that he could use for his paper. He looked over at Dan. Dan was taking notes from a book.

Clay wanted to sit with Dan. But some other boys were sitting with him, and there wasn't an extra chair.

Clay saw an empty table. He went over to it and sat down.

Clay saw Claire. Claire was in his math class. She was Kirk's girlfriend.

Claire sat at the table next to Clay.

She took notes from a book. But then she looked up and saw Clay.

She said, “Hi, Clay. Are you here to work on a science project for Mr. Young?”

“No. I’m working on an English paper for Mrs. Vance,” Clay said.

Clay read his book. And Claire took more notes.

Kim walked over to Claire.

She asked, “Did you find something we can use?”

“Yes. Did you?” Claire asked.

Clay wasn’t trying to hear what Kim said, but he couldn’t help it. She was standing near him.

Kim said, “I found a few things. But I think we need more. I don’t know where else to look. I will ask Mrs. Lin. Maybe she can help me.”

Kim didn't speak to Clay. But Clay didn't think Kim saw him.

Kim hurried over to Mrs. Lin. Mrs. Lin was the media center teacher.

A few minutes later, Kim came back over to Claire.

Kim said, "I asked Mrs. Lin. She said the library downtown might have the books we need."

Claire said, "We could go there on Saturday. Or you could come over to my house. Then we could work on our project. We could go to the library downtown next week. What do you want to do?"

"Can we go to the library on Saturday? Is that OK with you?" Kim asked.

Claire said, "Sure. I can meet you there. What time do you want to meet?"

“What about 2:00?” Kim asked.

“OK,” Claire said.

Kim sat down at the table. She saw Clay. She smiled at him.

She said, “Hi, Clay.”

“Hi,” Clay said.

Clay wished he had time to talk to Kim, but he didn’t. They both needed to work.

But Clay didn’t have any plans for Saturday. He would go to the library too. Then he would have time to talk to Kim.

Maybe she did want to date him. He would try to find out on Saturday.

Chapter 6

Clay worked in the media center until it was almost time for class. Then he went to class.

The morning went by quickly for Clay. And then it was time for lunch.

Clay went to the lunchroom. He got his tray.

Dan was sitting at a table. Dan waved to Clay. Clay went over to the table and sat down.

Dan asked, "Did you find what you needed this morning?"

"Yeah. Now I just have to write the paper. Did you find what you needed?" Clay asked.

Dan said, "Yeah. So now we can

really have fun writing our papers."

They knew it wouldn't be fun to write their papers, so they both laughed.

They ate lunch for a few minutes. And they didn't talk.

Then Dan said, "I wish we were playing Walker High for Homecoming. It should be an easy win for us."

"It should be," Clay said.

Dan said, "I wish we had next week off. Then we would have more time to get ready for the Hillman game. Why do we have to play Hillman for Homecoming? We should have an easy game for Homecoming."

Clay thought they should too.

Clay said, "But we can still beat Hillman. Besides, we know there will be one good thing about Homecoming."

"What?" Dan asked.

"The dance," Clay said.

"I don't know about that," Dan said.

Clay asked, "Why? Don't you want to go to the dance?"

"Yeah. But Eve hurt her foot in a volleyball game. She can't play in any more games. And I am not sure her foot will be OK by then. So she might not be able to dance," Dan said.

"You can always sit all night, and watch the rest of us dance," Clay said.

Dan said, "Yeah. I know. But that wouldn't be much fun."

"I might let you dance with my date. But only for one or two dances," Clay said.

Dan laughed.

Then he said, "No thanks. I don't think Eve would like that."

Clay was sure Dan was right about that.

"Who are you taking to the dance?" Dan asked.

"I don't know yet," Clay said.

He didn't know who he would ask, but he wanted to ask Kim. He hoped she didn't already have a date.

"You are going, aren't you?" Dan asked.

Clay said, "Sure. I plan to go. I just don't have a date yet."

"Kim doesn't have a boyfriend now. So why don't you ask her?" Dan asked.

"I might ask Kim. I will think about it. Who is Kirk going to take to the dance? Will he take Claire?" Clay asked.

Dan said, "I think so. But I am not sure. They are having some problems. Kirk hasn't asked her yet. He liked her a lot last year. But I don't think he likes her as much this year."

Then the boys talked about the Walker High game again. They didn't talk any more about the dance.

Chapter 7

It was Friday night. The Walker High game had just ended. Carter High had won 35–12.

Clay walked across the field. He was on his way to the locker room.

Some boys yelled to him. They said, "Great game, Clay."

Clay had thrown three passes for a touchdown.

"Thanks," Clay yelled back to them.

Clay saw Kim. She smiled at him and waved. He smiled back at her and waved.

Kim was with some girls. So Clay didn't think she had a date. But he wasn't sure.

Hank ran up to him.

Hank had played late in the game. He threw a few passes, but they weren't good passes.

Hank asked, "Is it OK for me to walk with you, Clay?"

"Sure," Clay said.

Hank said, "You played a great game, Clay."

"Thanks," Clay said.

Clay wanted to say Hank played well. But Hank knew he didn't play well. And Clay wouldn't lie to him. That wouldn't be fair to Hank.

Hank said, "I am glad the coach let me play. But I didn't play well. I wish I could pass like you do, Clay."

"Keep working on your passing. It takes a lot of hard work," Clay said.

"That is why I want to talk to you. I

want to ask you something," Hank said.

"What?" Clay asked.

At first Hank didn't answer.

But then he said, "I want to be the starting quarterback next year. So I need to learn a lot this year. And I need some extra help with my passing and with some of the plays. Will you help me?"

"Sure," Clay said.

He could find some time to help Hank at practice.

Hank said, "Great. How about tomorrow afternoon?"

That surprised Clay.

"We don't have practice then," Clay said.

Hank should know that.

Hank said, "I know. But I thought you could come over to my house.

Maybe you could help me there."

At first Clay didn't say anything.

He didn't want to help Hank on Saturday. He wanted to go to the library. Clay hoped to talk to Kim there.

Hank said, "It is OK. You don't have to help me. I shouldn't have asked you."

Clay wanted very much to see Kim. But he also knew how Hank must feel. Clay had needed help last year, and Dan had helped him. Dan helped Clay even though Clay might get the job he wanted.

Clay said, "Sure. I will help you with your passes. What time do you want me to be at your house?"

"Any time you say," Hank said.

"OK. How about 2:00?" Clay asked.

"Great," Hank said.

"Fine. I will see you then," Clay said.

But Clay wouldn't get a chance to see Kim. And he wanted very much to see her on Saturday.

Chapter 8

It was the next day. Clay got to Hank's house about 2:00.

Clay gave Hank some tips about how to pass. Then Hank threw some passes to him.

Hank was nice. Clay was glad he helped Hank. But he still wanted to be at the library and see Kim.

Clay and Hank worked for a long time.

Then Hank said, "It is hot out here. Do you want to go inside for a while? We could get something to drink. We could talk about some of the plays."

"Sure," Clay said.

The boys started to walk to the

house. But then Hank stopped.

He said, "I guess I should tell you something before we go in."

"What?" Clay asked.

Hank said, "My sister is in there with one of her friends. They are working on a project. I thought they were going to be at the library downtown. Then they wouldn't get in our way."

"That is OK," Clay said.

Hank said, "Good. I told Claire that you were coming over here to help me. So I don't know why they are working here, and not working at the library."

Clay was very surprised. He didn't know Claire was Hank's sister.

He asked, "Claire is your sister?"

"Yeah," Hank said.

Clay asked, "Who is her friend?"

Was it Kim? But it must be.

"Some girl in her science class. I think her name is Kim," Hank said.

Clay was glad to hear that.

"Did Kim know I was going to be here?" Clay asked.

"Yeah," Hank said.

"Are you sure?" Clay asked.

"Yeah. Claire told her. And then Claire said they were going to work here. Why?" Hank asked.

Clay didn't answer.

Hank laughed.

Then Hank said, "You must know Kim. Maybe she wanted to see you."

"Maybe," Clay said.

He sure hoped she did.

"And maybe you would like to see her," Hank said.

"Maybe," Clay said.

The boys went in the house. They went to the kitchen. Clay saw Kim and Claire. They were working at the kitchen table.

Kim said, “Hi, Clay.”

She gave him a big smile.

Kim did want to see him. Clay was sure of that.

Clay and Hank talked to the girls for a little while. Then they went back outside. The girls stayed in the kitchen. They studied hard on their project.

Hank worked on his passing some more. Then the boys talked about football plays.

Clay was in no hurry to go home.

Then Kim and Claire came outside. Kim had her books with her.

Kim said, “I have to go now. But I wanted to say good-bye.”

Hank said, “Clay has to go now too.

Maybe he could walk you home."

He looked over at Clay. And Clay knew what Hank was trying to do. He was trying to give Clay a chance to talk to Kim.

"Sure. Where do you live, Kim?" Clay asked.

Kim told him.

Clay and Kim quickly left. They walked to Kim's house.

"Thanks for walking me home, Clay. I am glad you were at Claire's house," Kim said.

"I am glad you were there too," Clay said.

"I don't get to see you much this year. I wish we saw each other more," Kim said.

"I wish we did too," Clay said.

Did Kim want him to ask her for a

date? Clay thought she did. And there was only one way to find out.

"Do you want to go out on a date sometime?" he asked.

"That would be great," Kim said.

So Clay hadn't been wrong. Kim did want to date him. But there was something he wanted to know.

"I asked you for a date last year. But you said no. Why did you change your mind?" Clay asked.

Kim said, "I didn't change my mind. I wanted to date you last year."

That surprised Clay very much.

Clay asked, "You did? Then why did you say no when I asked you?"

Kim said, "I said no because my best friend, Fran, liked you. But she has moved away. And she has a boyfriend at her new school. So it is OK to date you now."

Clay knew Fran had liked him. But he didn't know that was why Kim had said no.

Clay knew he was going to ask Kim to the Homecoming Dance. And he was sure she would say yes if she didn't have a date. He hoped it wasn't too late to ask her.

Clay said, "The Homecoming Dance is next week. Do you have a date for it?"

"No," Kim said.

"Do you want to go with me?" Clay asked.

"That would be great. I sure am glad Claire and I studied at her house. I'm glad I got to see you," Kim said.

Clay laughed.

He said, "I had planned to go to the library too. I thought you would be there, and I wanted to ask you for a date."

"Then why did you go to Claire's house? You didn't know I would be there," Kim said.

"Hank asked me to help him with his passes. And I didn't want to tell him no. Why did you study at Claire's house, and not at the library?" Clay asked.

At first Kim didn't answer.

But then she said, "Claire said you would be at her house. That is why I met Claire at her house. I hoped I could talk to you. I hoped you would ask me for a date."

Then they both laughed.

Clay knew this year was going to be a very good year.